For Conrad and Enzo with much love
xx VF

For Chris with love
CF

ORCHARD BOOKS
338 Euston Road, London NW1 3BH
Orchard Books Australia
Level 17/207, Kent Street, Sydney, NSW 2000
First published in Great Britain in 2007
First paperback publication 2008
Text © copyright Vivian French 2007
Illustrations © copyright Chris Fisher 2007
The rights of Vivian French and Chris Fisher to be
identified as the author and illustrator of this work
have been asserted by them in accordance with
the Copyright, Designs and Patents Act, 1988.

A CIP catalogue record for this book is
available from the British Library.

ISBN 978 1 84362 699 2 (hardback)
ISBN 978 1 84362 708 1 (paperback)

1 3 5 7 9 10 8 6 4 2 (hardback)
1 3 5 7 9 10 8 6 4 2 (paperback
Printed in Great Britain by
Antony Rowe Ltd, Chippenham, Wiltshire
Orchard Books is a division of Hachette Children's Books,
an Hachette Livre UK company.
www.orchardbooks.co.uk

DRAGLINS IN DANGER!

VIVIAN FRENCH   CHRIS FISHER

ORCHARD BOOKS

CHAPTER ONE

"**A** Chat?" Daffodil's eyes sparkled. "A real chat? And it's near here? Can we go and see it? Can we go now?"

Uncle Damson frowned. "Certainly NOT, Daffodil. All sensible draglins—" he paused to glare at his niece, "—treat chats with the most extreme care and caution. If you had paid *any* attention to me in the past, you would remember me telling you that I myself was once unlucky enough to have met one. The result was TERRIBLE." And Uncle Damson solemnly turned his back on his nieces and nephews to demonstrate his lack of tail.

Daffodil caught Dennis's eye, and the two of them shook with giggles. Danny tried hard to keep a straight face. Dora began to wail.

"Oh NOOOOOO! I was just beginning to like it here…and now we're all going to be eaten!"

"We are NOT going to be eaten, Dora," Aunt Plum said sharply. "But Uncle Puddle has heard wowling, and we do need to be careful. I think the four of you should stay inside until the coast is clear."

"It won't be for long," Uncle Puddle said comfortingly. "These things happen from time to time. Chats wander into the area, but they soon go away again."

"I know! We could trap it!" Daffodil said.

"And then what would you do with it?" Danny wanted to know.

Daffodil looked blank, then grinned. "I'd tame it, of course. And then we could use it to chase all the other chats and dawgs away."

"But dawgs chase chats," Danny argued. "Aunt Plum told us. Dawgs chase chats, chats chase mowsers, mowsers chase – what do mowsers chase, Aunt Plum?"

Dennis decided it was time to interrupt. "*Our* chat will be a FIERCE chat with long gnashy teeth!"

Dora clutched at Aunt Plum. "But I don't WANT a chat. Aunt Plum, tell them we can't have one!"

Aunt Plum folded her arms. "You're all being ridiculous," she said. "Chats are very VERY dangerous, and you must never think they aren't, but I'm sure this'll just turn out to be a scare. Now, if you can't think of anything else to do you can go and tidy your bedrooms."

CHAPTER TWO

"**I**'m bored," said Danny. It was the following day, and he was sprawled on the sitting room floor. Dennis was stretched out beside him, and Daffodil was flopped on a pile of thistledown cushions. Only Dora was sitting upright. She was trying to teach herself to knit with a twist of wool and two rusty pins that had once belonged to Human Beanies, but she wasn't finding it easy.

"Me too," said Daffodil. "I'm VERY bored."

"Huh!" Dennis tweaked her ankle. "I bet you're not as bored as I am. I'm the MOST BORED DRAGLIN IN THE WHOLE WIDE WORLD!"

"No you're NOT!" Daffodil never liked to be beaten by anyone, especially Dennis.

"NO ONE could be as bored as me." She picked up a cushion and whacked Dennis over the head. The cushion split, and thistledown floated everywhere.

"Wheeeee!" Daffodil shouted, and began to blow as hard as she could.

At once Dennis and Danny jumped up and joined in, and Dora was surrounded by a whirling storm of soft white down. "ATCHOO!" she sneezed. "ATCHOO!"

"WHATEVER is going on in here?"

Aunt Plum was standing in the doorway.

"Oops!" Daffodil said cheerfully. "Sorry, Aunt Plum. The cushion just sort of collapsed, and all this stuff came whooshing out of it. We were trying to catch it and put it back."

Aunt Plum turned to Dora. "What REALLY happened?"

Dora shook her head. "I don't know, Auntie. I wasn't looking. I was trying to get my knitting to work, and it was all going wrong."

Aunt Plum sighed. "I'll fetch a dustpan and brush. I know it's difficult for you being stuck indoors, but DO remember this isn't our house. Uncle Plant said this morning that the hallway was so full of junk he couldn't find his Collecting Bag."

"It's not JUNK," Dennis said indignantly. "It's our collection of Useful Things!"

"And it was Uncle Plant who said we couldn't bring it in the sitting room," Daffodil pointed out.

Danny nodded in agreement. "And YOU said we couldn't keep any more sticks and stones in our bedroom, Aunt Plum."

"We haven't been here a month," Aunt Plum said, "but if you bring in one more thing there'll be no room for any of us."

The four little draglins looked at each other. They were still getting used to the wonders of Outdoors. All their lives they had been cooped up in Under Roof at the top of tall, high flats, but now they had escaped, and their world was spilling over with all sorts of strange and exciting things.

Aunt Plum understood how they were feeling. "I know it's hard," she said. "Look, why don't you go and find a proper place for your Collections?" She paused, and went on. "I've got an idea. I think you'll be safe as long as you keep to Under Shed. This house only takes up a tiny part of it. If you go past the mowsers' hole, and the box shed where Daffodil keeps Speedy, you'll find masses of space. Just don't interfere with any of the uncles' things. And promise you WON'T go any further into Outdoors!"

"WOW!" Dennis was thrilled. "Our very own Collecting Store!"

"Can we have a space each?" Daffodil wanted to know.

"Oh YES!" Dora's eyes shone as she tidied her knitting into her pocket.

Aunt Plum smiled. "Why don't we see if we can find a Collecting Place for each of you? After all, you are draglins, and Collecting is what draglins do best. I'm sure Uncle Plant and Uncle Puddle will think it's a very good idea. Especially if it clears out the hall…"

"Hurrah!" Dennis, Danny, Dora and Daffodil clapped loudly.

"I'll just check that Pip's still asleep in his cot," Aunt Plum told them, "and then I'll be with you. Oh, and I expect this sitting room to be SPOTLESS by the time the uncles come home this evening. Deal?"

"DEAL!" chorused the draglins.

CHAPTER THREE

Aunt Plum was right. Uncle Plant and Uncle Puddle's house was carefully hidden under a broken down old shed that had originally been built by Human Beanies. No Beanies had been near for years now, and the shed had all but collapsed, but the floor was still sound and protected from the damp ground by pillars of brick. It made a substantial ceiling for the house, and gave the uncles a large sheltered storage area.

"WOW!" Dennis, Danny, Dora and Daffodil stared round, their eyes wide. Uncle Plant and Uncle Puddle had been busy; there were neat piles of twigs for firewood, heaps of dried berries, a collection of bits of metal including several pins, and a host of other bits and pieces all arranged in tidy rows.

Even so there was still a good deal of unused space, and Dennis rushed forward with a yell of triumph. "Bags I this bit here!" he shouted. "We can mark it out. Danny, can you find a stick?"

"SH!" Aunt Plum said, as she looked over her shoulder. "You mustn't shout, Dennis. It may feel safe under here, but there's always the chance the chat might still be prowling about."

"NO probs!" Daffodil dashed to the metal collection and seized a bent darning needle. "I'll see it off!"

"Daffodil!" Aunt Plum looked cross. "What did I say? No shouting. And put that back AT ONCE!"

"Oh...all right." Daffodil grudgingly put the needle back. "Dor, can I have your knitting pins?"

Dora shook her head. "I want to knit Ruby a scarf."

"A scarf for a mowser?" Daffodil made a face. "OK, I'll find my OWN weapons.

And I'll have that big space next to Dennis because I'm going to have the BIGGEST Collection ever."

Dora moved close to Aunt Plum. Her heart was beating fast, but she didn't want Dennis and Danny and Daffodil to know how scared she was. "Aunt Plum," she whispered, "would a chat fit under here? Wouldn't it be much too big?"

Aunt Plum squeezed her hand. "Probably."

"PROBABLY?" Dora squealed. "You mean it MIGHT? Oh NO! Oh, Aunt Plum – I don't want a space out here – I really don't!"

"What's the matter, Dor?" Danny asked.

Dora burst into tears. "Aunt Plum says the chat could get under here and eat us all up!" she sobbed." We should go back inside! Oh, I DO so wish we were back in lovely cosy Under Roof."

"I don't," Danny said. "You saw the beanies working up there, just like we all did. We'd have been discovered for certain. And it would have to be a REALLY teensy weensy chat to get under here, Dor – we'd hear it coming a mile off."

"But we might not," Daffodil said hopefully. "It might come creeping up on its silent chatty feet and—"

"DAFFODIL!" Aunt Plum said. "Why do you think the uncles have put dry leaves and twigs all round Under Shed? Of COURSE we'd hear it coming."

Dora blew her nose. "Are you sure, Aunt Plum?"

"QUITE sure. Now go with Danny, and pick a nice spot to keep your feathers in.

Dennis and Daffodil will grab the whole space otherwise. I'm going back inside to see if Pip's woken up yet."

Aunt Plum stood and watched Danny drag Dora in between the pillars. It was a pity Uncle Puddle had heard a chat this week, she thought. Dora had been so much braver after her adventure rescuing the wash bag.

Besides, it was most probably a false alarm. Aunt Plum smiled as she went into the house. The little draglins would be quite safe Under Shed, she was sure.

CHAPTER FOUR

For an hour or two, Dennis, Danny, Daffodil and Dora were quite happy. They trailed to and from the house to the store with their Collections, and Aunt Plum was delighted to see how empty Uncle Puddle's hallway was looking.

"There's LOADS of space still," Dennis said happily as he put down the last of his sticks. "We could have the biggest Collection ever!"

"We could build a house to keep it in," Danny suggested.

Dora looked up from her feathers. "Or we could build a play house," she said. "Just for us!"

"PLAY house?" Daffodil sniffed. "We're not babies, Dor." She jumped up. "I think we should have a racetrack! We could have AMAZING races!"

"Brilliant!" Dennis punched the air. "We could race the mowsers!"

Dora looked anxious. "But Ruby's so little."

"We can race Hero," Daffodil said. "It would give her some exercise! She's EVER so fat!"

"How can we race her when there's nothing for her to race against?" Danny asked.

Daffodil glared at him. "Danny Draglin, you are SO boring! I'LL race her! And I'll win!"

Danny shrugged. "If you say so. But Hero can go really fast if she wants to."

"And you can't run for toffee," Dennis said.

"Yes I can!" Daffodil's face was getting redder and redder. "Bet I can beat you! Bet you my whole Collection I can beat you AND Danny AND Dora!"

"You're on," said Dennis.

"Yeah!" said Danny.

"Can I say 'Ready steady go'?" Dora asked.

"No!" Daffodil yelled.

The four draglins hurried past the uncles' Collections and lined up, ready to race.

Daffodil pointed to where a twist of ivy was creeping in from the daylight on the far side of Under Shed. "First one to touch the leaves is the winner," she announced. "Ready – go!" And she was off.

Dennis, Dora and Danny were taken by surprise. Dennis opened his mouth to protest, but then Danny stormed past him, with Dora close behind. Dennis gritted his teeth and RAN. He passed Dora easily, and with a huge effort he was past Danny.

On and on he and Danny ran, with Daffodil always just ahead. She had very nearly won when she made the mistake of looking over her shoulder.

"Da da de da da! Can't catch me!" she shouted, tripped, and fell.

Dennis tore past Daffodil into the daylight...and crashed straight into soft fur, with steely muscle and hard bone beneath.

"YIKES!" yelled Dennis.

"YEEEEEOWL!" howled the cat.

Dennis spun round, and ran for safety.

"Come on, Dennis! FASTER! YOU CAN DO IT!" Danny shrieked as Dennis panted towards him...

ZONK! An enormous paw swiped at Dennis. The sharp yellowing claws, each as long as a draglin's hand, caught his shirt.

For a second Dennis hung dangling…and then he disappeared.

Daffodil struggled to her feet. "QUICK!" she shouted. "Follow him!"

CHAPTER FIVE

I f anyone had ever told Dora she would find herself chasing after a cat, she would probably have fainted. Now that it was happening, she was so terrified of what might happen to Dennis she had no time to think of anything else. She and Danny and Daffodil tore over the tufts of grass, desperately trying to keep their brother in view.

They were puffing hard, and all but at their last gasp when the cat finally stopped. The ground was rough with thistles and brambles, and they were close to a clump of thorny bushes in front of an old brick wall.

The cat stood still, and Danny, peering from behind a thistle stalk, could see its tattered ears flicking to and fro.

"Sh! It's listening!" he mouthed.

The cat turned its head, and for a moment Danny, Daffodil and Dora found themselves looking straight into its narrowed yellow eyes. Dennis was hanging from its mouth by the back of his shirt.

As the others stared, Dennis began to wriggle and kick and shout, and the cat lowered its head and dropped him. Keeping him pinned down with a paw, it began to make a strange m'rup! m'rup! noise.

To the horror of the watching draglins, three more cats came creeping out from a hole under a hawthorn bush. They were much smaller, and wobbly on their legs, but they were licking their lips with tiny pink tongues.

"LOOK!" Danny breathed. "Chatterlets! And I think Dennis is meant to be their dinner!"

"We'll see about that!" Daffodil muttered.

"Oh NO! What's happened to Dennis?" Dora gasped. "Look! He's lying so still!"

It was true. The cat had removed her paw, but Dennis was lying limply, not moving a muscle. The big cat sniffed him, then pushed him. Dennis didn't respond. The kittens ignored him and staggered towards their mother.

"What are we going to DO?" Daffodil hissed. "We've got to do SOMETHING!"

As if in answer, there was the faint sound of a dog barking in the distance. The cat leapt up and stared fiercely round, and the kittens hurried to their hiding place. Dennis stayed where he was.

The cat sniffed him once more, then in one fluid leap she was on the wall, staring out into the distance, the fur on her spine bristling and her whiskers twitching.

"NOW!" shouted Daffodil. "GET DENNIS!" and she jumped out from the thistles...

"SH!" Danny hissed. He flung himself at Daffodil. For the second time that day she fell flat on her face.

The cat swivelled. She saw Danny and Daffodil, and her yellow eyes gleamed. She poised herself to spring, her body quivering – and the barking came again, this time louder.

"Woof woof woof WOOF!"

For a second the cat couldn't decide what to do. She looked first one way, then the other. Danny grabbed Dora's hand, and pulled her and Daffodil into the nearest brambles. "DOWN!" he ordered, and they burrowed as deep as they could under the knotted and thorny branches.

A couple of metres away Dennis seized the opportunity to dive into the twiggy roots of the bushes and wriggle his way to the bottom of the wall. "There's sure to be a gap somewhere," he told himself. "Or I can creep along here until I get far enough away from the chat to climb up and see where I am. I can do it. I KNOW I can…" And then he saw it. A hole in the bricks. A draglin-sized hole.

He crept inside, his heart racing, and found it was only the size of a missing half brick. One scoop of a cat's paw, and he'd be caught.

34

The thought was hardly in his mind before the cat landed with a THUD! There was a slithering, and the rustle of leaves, and a cruel glittering eye peered in at him. Then came the paw, with the claws as sharp as razors—

"Typical Under Roofer," said a voice, and Dennis was grabbed by his shirt collar and whisked upwards into darkness.

CHAPTER SIX

"**O**W!" Daffodil said, as loudly as she dared. "It's really prickly under these horrid brambles!"

"You're jolly lucky you aren't being EATEN!" Danny said furiously. "Just how STUPID can you be, Daffy? That chat SAW us because of you!"

There was a moment's pause while Daffodil tried hard to think of a crushing answer, and couldn't.

"We should think about what to do next," Dora suggested. "Do you think we should go home, and get the uncles and Aunt Plum?"

Danny waited for Daffodil to say she was going to deal with the chat single-handed, but for once she was quiet.

"You might be right, Dor," he said. "What do you think, Daffy?"

"I want to know if Dennis is OK. I'm not going anywhere until I know that." Daffodil was subdued, but determined.

To Danny's surprise, Dora nodded. "Me too," she said. "And you know we heard that dawg? Maybe it'll chase the chat away, and then we can all go home together."

Daffodil gave an enthusiastic squeal. "WOW, Dor! That's brilliant! Hey! THAT'S IT! We find the dawg, and get it to chase us, and lead it here to chase the chat!" At once Daffodil began struggling out from her thorny hidey-hole.

Danny groaned. "Hang on – just HANG ON! Aren't you forgetting something?"

"What NOW?" His sister glared at him.

"The dawg's on the other side of the wall," Danny said. "Dawgs can't climb."

"Oh." Daffodil sat down again. "Maybe we could find a way round?"

Danny shook his head. "I don't think so," he said.

"Oh, POOR Dennis." Daffodil sniffed loudly, and wiped her nose with the back of her hand.

Dora automatically fished in her pocket for the little clean hankie she always carried, and pricked herself on one of her knitting pins. "Ouch," she said, but Danny and Daffodil were too wrapped up in their own thoughts to notice her.

Dora sucked her finger quietly.

CHAPTER SEVEN

Dennis coughed, and rubbed his neck. His sudden rescue had saved him from the cat, but had almost strangled him.

"Make all the noise you want," said the voice that had spoken before. "She can't touch you here, can she, Rigger?"

There was no answer.

"He's shaking his head," the voice informed Dennis.

Dennis peered through the gloom, and the shape of a tall thin draglin gradually became clear. The draglin was nodding, so he decided that must be Rigger.

"I'm Rick," said the voice. "And you must be one of the Under Roofers. Uncle Plant said you were coming. Said we were to look out for you, as you were bound to get into trouble."

Dennis turned, and saw that Rick was Rigger's twin.

"Hi," he said. "I'm Dennis. Erm...thanks for saving me. And you too, Rigger."

"No probs," Rick said. Rigger grinned.

Dennis suddenly realised he was on a narrow shelf just above the gap in the bricks where he had tried to hide. On either side, on the same level as the shelf, a tunnel stretched away into the darkness. "Are we INSIDE the wall?" he asked.

"Certainly are," Rick said. "Been in the Underground?"

"Of course I have," Dennis said indignantly. "I had a real adventure—"

Rick cut him off. "OK. Well, THIS is the OVERground. Goes everywhere the wall goes. Doesn't it, Rigger?"

Rigger nodded.

Dennis was annoyed Rick hadn't let him tell him about his adventures, and it made him rude. "Doesn't Rigger ever say anything?" he asked. "What's wrong with him?"

Rick slapped him. Dennis jumped. "OUCH!" he said. "What was THAT for?"

"Don't you EVER say anything bad about my brother," Rick growled. "If it weren't for Rigger you'd be a chat's dinner by now! Show him, Rigger!"

"Woof! Woof woof woof WOOF!"

The barking was so realistic that Dennis clutched Rick's arm.

The cat, who had been waiting outside the hole where her prey had vanished, flattened her ears and fled away to her kittens.

On the far side of the bushes, in among the brambles, Danny, Daffodil and Dora looked at each other in alarm.

43

"WOW!" Dennis breathed. "That is SO clever! Could you teach me to do that?"

"It's a gift," Rick told him. "Only Rigger's got it. Isn't that right, Rig?"

Rigger beamed happily. "WOOF!"

"Right," Rick said. "Got to get this little Under Roofer home to his ma. Ready, young Dennis? Better hold on to my tail."

"Just a minute," Dennis said angrily. "Stop treating me like a baby! I appreciate your saving me, but my brother and sisters are out there somewhere, and I've got to find them. And—" he folded his arms and stared hard at Rick, "—I haven't GOT a mother, as it happens. I live with my uncle and aunt. So there."

Dennis half expected Rick to slap him again, but instead the older draglin roared with laughter. Rigger laughed too.

"Good for you," Rick said. "You're standing up for your folks, and that's fine by me."

There was a rumbling noise from Rigger.

Rick glanced at him.

"You're right, Rig. He says you did good when you played dead for the chat, kid."

"Oh! Er – thanks." Dennis swelled with pride. "Did you see me? Did it look real?"

"Yup." Rick waved a hand dismissively. "Now, we've got to make a plan. What do you think, Rigger? Think we should take the Stair to Heaven?"

Rigger nodded.

"Great," Rick said. "Can you climb, kid?"

"Of COURSE I can," Dennis told him. "I'm an ACE climber! When I was—"

Rick didn't want to know. "Sure, sure. Whatever. Come on – let's go!"

CHAPTER EIGHT

As Dennis toiled up the Stair to Heaven he couldn't help wishing he hadn't been so boastful. The stair wasn't a stair at all, but a series of gaps in between the bricks, like a remarkably crooked chimney in an old house. He had to use his knees and elbows as the space was extremely narrow, and they were soon rubbed red and raw.

Rick and Rigger, already far ahead of him, dislodged small pebbles and crumbs of mortar as they climbed, and Dennis quickly learnt to keep his mouth closed. Finally there was a faint glimmer, then a ray of sunlight, and Dennis was able to heave himself out and on to the top of the wall. Rick and Rigger were standing side by side scanning the garden below. There was no sign of the cat.

"WOW!" Dennis said as he saw how high they were. "WOW! I can see for MILES! Oh – look – there's Under Shed! And—" he squinted at the tenement block at the top of the garden. "That's where I used to live when we were Under Roof! Only it's all different now…"

"We're not here for the view, kid," Rick said, but not unkindly. "See if you can see your folks anywhere. Rigger's watching out for the chat. She's down there with her chatterlets, but if she sees us she'll be up like a shot."

Dennis studied the garden. He was pleased to see just how much distance lay between Under Shed and the tenement where the Beanies lived, and how the trees and straggling shrubs and brambles blocked the disused pathways. A tiny movement caught his eye, and he leant forward.

"Careful," Rick said. "Won't help nothing if you fall off!"

Dennis didn't answer. He was staring so hard his eyes hurt. Was it a movement? Was something stirring among the brambles? "Rick," he said, "can you see anything? Just down there – there's a clump of thistles, and then there's a whole heap of brambles – and I think they might be there, but I can't be sure…"

Rick fished in his pocket and pulled out a spyglass. He twirled it expertly, and put it to his eye. "Let's see. No…no…no…YES! I can see a girl draglin – and a bit of another – can't see what sort, though – and YES! There's another! You're right, kid. They're in the brambles. What's the chat up to, Rig?"

Rigger rumbled softly.

"Can't see any sign of her? Well, why don't we take a risk. Rigger – let's have one of your best whistles. Put your hands over your ears, kid – it's LOUD!"

Dennis did as he was told, but even so

Rigger's whistle tore through his head like a slicing blade.

"They heard that all right," Rick said.

He handed the spyglass to Dennis.

"Popped their heads up straight away. Typical Under Roofers."

Dennis, peering through the glass, couldn't help smiling.

He could see Danny trying to make Daffodil keep down, and it was very obvious that Daffodil was arguing. Dora looked as if she was staring straight at him, and he waved. To his amazement she waved back, and then said something to the others.

"Uh uh," Rick said, his eyes screwed up to see better. "You know what, kid? We've made a BIG mistake. They're getting up. Oh no…don't tell me they're going to make a run for it this way. They aren't THAT stupid…or are they?"

Dennis, still looking through the glass, said, "Erm…looks like Daffodil is. And Danny. AND Dora."

CHAPTER NINE

Dora had tried her best. "Just because Dennis is waving doesn't mean that it's safe for us," she said. "It really, really doesn't. He's just showing us he's all right…"

"You know what, Dor? You're worse than Aunt Plum," Daffodil said scathingly.

"Dora might be right, though." Danny rubbed his nose. "I mean, Dennis is OK up there – well, as long as the chat doesn't see him – but WE'RE on her level! And she's already seen us once – she knows we're here."

"He waved to tell us it was safe. I KNOW he did!" Daffodil pushed her way past the last bramble stem. "Besides, I want to see those other draglins!" And she began to run.

"We can't let her go on her own," Danny said despairingly, and charged after her. Dora, wringing her hands, ran after him.

*

The draglins on top of the wall watched in silence. Dennis had a sick feeling at the pit of his stomach as he saw his brother and sisters getting closer to the hawthorn bush that hid the cat and her kittens from view. Various wild plans swirled round his brain, but none seemed to make sense. "If Rigger whistled again, we could tell them to go back," was the best he could think of.

Rick raised an eyebrow. "What – have a shouting match? Don't you think the chat would notice?"

It was as if Daffodil had heard him. She stopped in front of the hawthorn. "DENNIS! WE'RE COMING!" she yelled. "WE'LL CLIMB THE WALL! SEE YOU IN A MINUTE!"

Then three things happened at once.

Rigger rumbled an urgent warning.

The cat leapt at Daffodil.

Dennis jumped from the top of the wall.

There was a yowling, spitting, hissing

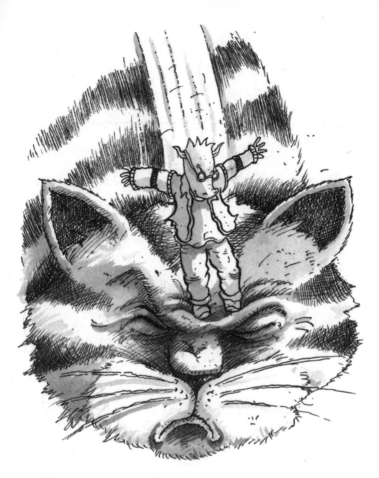

confusion – and the cat was gone.

"WOW!" said Danny. "Did you hear the 'CLUNK!' as Dennis landed?"

Dora shook her head. "All I heard was wowling. Poor thing...it must have had an awful shock."

"Dora!" Daffodil was appalled. "It was

a CHAT! And besides, it didn't run away because of Dennis. It ran away because I made a face at it!"

"That's such RUBBISH!" Dennis said. "You ask Rick and Rigger! They'll tell you!"

"Who are Rick and Rigger?" Danny asked. "Are they the draglins on the wall?"

Dennis nodded. "They'll be here in a minute."

Dora suddenly burst into floods of tears.

"Whatever's the matter, Dor?" Daffodil asked. "We're all safe, and I've got rid of the chat. We can go home now. Well – just as soon as I've said hello to Rick and – what did you say his name was, Dennis?"

Daffodil couldn't hear Dennis answer. Dora was crying too loudly. "I was so worried about Dennis," she sobbed, "and now we've found him, but we're still miles from home and that chat'll be really, really, REALLY angry with us now, and we shouldn't be standing here when it might come back any minute! And even if it doesn't come back it's still here in the garden, and what we should be doing is getting rid of it for EVER!"

As Dennis, Danny and Daffodil stared helplessly at Dora, Rick and Rigger appeared behind them. "She's right, you know," Rick said. "Isn't she right, Rig?"

Rigger rumbled something.

"Just what I was thinking, Rigger," Rick said, and he turned to Dennis. "If that chat's got chatterlets, they'll be getting bigger and hungrier every day. If they stay around here we'll end up with FOUR chats. And there's a load of happy little draglins living in these here parts." He punched Dennis on the arm. "You up for some action, kid?"

Dennis glowed. "Count me in," he said proudly.

"AND me," Daffodil pushed forward. "After all, it WAS me that got rid of the chat."

Rick frowned. "Look," he said. "This is serious stuff. If you think you can scare a great big chat by pulling a silly face you might as well go home now. Rigger'll see you there safely, won't you, Rig?"

Rigger nodded.

Daffodil's face went an alarmingly bright purple. Dora, sitting up and wiping her nose, waited for the storm.

Daffodil swallowed hard, several times. "OK," she said at last. "I take it back. It was Dennis. But I do want to help get rid of the chats. PLEASE?"

Rick raised his eyebrows at Dennis. Dennis, quivering with self-importance, turned to his gang. "You can help. But just make sure you do EVERYTHING Rick and Rigger tell you. All right?"

Danny, Dora and Daffodil nodded mutely and got up to follow the others.

CHAPTER TEN

The council of war was held back in the Overground, on the narrow shelf inside the wall.

"I think we should all listen to Rick and Rigger," Dennis said as soon as everyone was sitting down. "They know MUCH more about chats than we do." And he sat back, waiting for Rick to tell him he was right.

Instead, Rick looked at Dora and Danny. "What do YOU reckon?"

"I don't think we can ever get rid of the chat completely," Danny said slowly. "But if we could somehow drive her away from this end of the garden that would help."

"Good point," Rick said. "That chat's been around for years, off and on. Hasn't she, Rigger? Must belong to some Beanies in the flats. But she's only been trouble round here for the last few weeks."

"That's because she's got chatterlets," Dora said in her soft little voice. "If we could move them, she'd go too."

"That's so STUPID, Dor!" Daffodil burst out. "What we need to do is attack her! Pull her wickers out! Set fire to—"

Rick held up his hand and Daffodil, seeing his expression, stopped.

"I thought you Under Roofers didn't know anything," Rick said. "But I was wrong!" He patted Dora's back. "You've got it in one, kid. Sharp as a tack, isn't she, Rigger?"

Rigger beamed so broadly that Dora blushed.

"Those chatterlets are still teensy," Rick went on. "They've got teeth and claws, but they're wobbly on their feet, and they don't see too well yet. I reckon if we could get their ma out of the way for a bit we could block up their hidey-hole so's they can't get in. She'll take them somewhere else then, because she'll need to know they're safe."

"Oh dear," Dora said sadly.

"What's the matter, kid?" Rick asked. "You see a problem?"

Dora shook her head. "No," she said. "I'm sorry. It just made me think of POOR Aunt Plum. We've been missing for AGES, and she'll be ever so worried."

Rigger gave a particularly loud rumble.

"Don't you fret, kid," Rick said. "Rigger'll whistle to her. She'll know you're safe with us then."

"Thank you," Dora said politely. She had no idea what Rick meant, but it sounded kind, and she was grateful.

Dennis dug her with his elbow. "Rigger can whistle SUPER loud," he whispered. "Aunt Plum'll hear it even if she's in the house!"

"But how will she know what it means?" Dora whispered back.

Rick had heard her. "Your aunt's my mum's sister," he explained. "They all understand Whistle. Hasn't she taught you lot yet?"

The four little draglins shook their heads.

"H'm," Rick said. "Well, listen to Rigger. He's the best ever! Hands over ears though!"

Rigger stood up and moved nearer the entrance to the Overground. The draglins heard him give three long and four short whistles before he came back, grinning happily. "She'll be fine now," Rick told them. "And now – let's go! Rigger, can you stay here and get that big chat away from the chatterlets, and then keep her busy? She'll still be feeling woozy from when wonder boy here jumped on her head, so hopefully she won't be thinking straight."

Rigger nodded.

"And the rest of us'll deal with the chatterlets. Everyone OK with that?"

"Could I stay with Rigger?" Dora asked. "Or would I get in his way?"

Rigger gave a happy rumble, and Dora smiled at him.

Dennis, Danny and Daffodil saluted smartly. "Ready," they said.

"Right!" said their leader. "Rig, we'll whistle when we've blocked the hole. And now – let's GO!"

CHAPTER ELEVEN

As Rick and the three younger draglins slid out of the narrow shelf in the Overground and tiptoed away, Rigger began counting on his fingers. When he had reached thirty he stood up, and balanced himself over the half brick opening where Dennis had found shelter. Dora, watching, could only guess at what he was up to – and then she heard him. He began with a series of agonised howls, and then mewed piteously. The hollow space in the tunnel made the sound echo, and Dora thought she had never heard such sad little cries.

There was a scrabbling sound. Dora held her breath. A paw appeared in the space below, and as Rigger continued his kitten-in-distress noises the mother cat began to answer with soft little murmuring sounds.

Rigger touched Dora's hand and pointed, without stopping his plaintive mewling. The cat now had two paws in the hole, and was scratching at the brick.

Dora shuddered as she saw the scimitar claws. "AAGH!"

Without warning, a paw had scooped upwards, and caught Rigger's foot. He yelled loudly, and fell – and in the distance Dora heard a high-pitched whistle.

She took a deep breath. "Dora! Be brave!" she said, and scrambled after Rigger.

The cat was pulling him towards her, her ears back and her tail twitching.

"She thinks he's hidden one of her chatterlets," Dora thought, and as she pulled the steel knitting pins from her pocket, she looked up. "I'm SORRY," she said, shut her eyes, and stabbed wildly.

The cat had had enough. She had been pushed, jumped on, and now her paw was stinging. She let out a yeowl, and ran...and found her kittens meowing pathetically outside their hole, which was now blocked with brambles and broken sticks. The cat seized the nearest kitten by the scruff of the neck, and set off for the tenement. There was, she was almost sure, a convenient warm cellar at the bottom of the block...and the sooner she got this

kitten there, the sooner she could collect the other two.

Rick, Danny, Dennis and Daffodil came dashing up to where Dora was inspecting Rigger's foot. There was a nasty scratch, but Dora wrapped it carefully in her little white hankie.

"Whatever happened?" Rick asked. "And why did that chat go belting off like that?"

Rigger began to rumble excitedly, but for once Dora spoke first. "Nothing much," she said. "Just teamwork. And now I think we'd better get home. Aunt Plum will be waiting for us."

CHAPTER TWELVE

Dora was right. When the six draglins reached Under Shed, Aunt Plum was standing outside the gate. Uncle Damson was behind her, with Pip, and Uncle Puddle and Uncle Plant were by the doorway.

"THERE you are," Aunt Plum said. She rushed forward to hug all six draglins, and when she had finished she hugged them all over again.

"Rick, Rigger," she said at last, "I can't thank you enough for saving Dennis and Danny and Daffy and Dora! They were very, VERY naughty to go out – who KNOWS what might have happened to them if you hadn't found them?"

Rick grinned. "Actually, Aunt Plum," he said, "they were OK. And we sort of teamed up to sort out the chat problem.

She won't be around so much, now. That's right, isn't it, Rigger?"

Rigger beamed.

Aunt Plum went very pale. "They've been near a CHAT?"

"Sorted her good and proper," Rick said cheerfully. "Dennis jumped on her head, and Dora stuck pins in her paw."

Aunt Plum stared at him aghast, but Uncle Damson gave a sudden gasp, and doubled up with laughter. Uncle Puddle rocked to and fro chortling loudly, and Uncle Plant shook all over as he ho ho ho'd and hee hee hee'd.

"What a STORY!" Uncle Damson said as he wiped his streaming eyes. "Dennis jumping on a chat's head is good, but as for Dora sticking it with pins! Goodness me!" He wiped his eyes again, and slapped Rick on the back. "Well I never! You know, if I thought even a WORD of that was true I'd put them under lock and key for ever to keep them safe!"

Dennis, Danny, Daffodil and Dora stared at him in horror.

"But—" said Daffodil.

"You couldn't—" said Dennis.

"What—" said Danny.

"We didn't—" said Dora.

"You know what, Uncle Plum," Rick said loudly. "It's a good thing they're all as good as gold." And he winked at his four little cousins. So did Rigger.

Dennis, Danny and Daffodil winked back, but Dora noticed Aunt Plum inspecting

Rick and Rigger thoughtfully.

"OH! Aunt PLUM!" she squealed. "I'm so SORRY! We haven't cleared up the thistledown! We were just saying we'd do it the minute we got back…weren't we?" She elbowed Danny, who nodded hard.

"That's right," Danny said. "We said we'd have a good clean and tidy-up, didn't we Daffodil?"

"Did we?" Daffodil asked blankly.

Rick grinned at Uncle Damson and Aunt Plum. "What did I tell you? Good as gold! Now, we don't want to get in the way of you lot tidying, do we, Rigger? See you, kids!"

And the two teenage draglins marched away, whistling loudly.

"Right," Aunt Plum said. "In you come. You're quite right, Dora. That thistledown needs sorting." As the draglins walked inside, Aunt Plum put her arm round Dora's shoulders. "Poor little Dora," she said. "I do hope you weren't too scared… but I've got some good news for you. The uncles and I have made a decision. We can't have the four of you running around Outdoors." She shook her head. "I know you're a good sweet stay-at-home little draglin, and Danny's very sensible at heart, but we're worried about Dennis and Daffodil. We can't risk them leading you into trouble, and something terrible happening. I mean, WHATEVER would you do if you came face to face with a chat? So we're going to send you all to school. You'll start next week…"

by Vivian French
illustrated by Chris Fisher

All priced at £8.99.

Draglins books are available from all good bookshops,
or can be ordered direct from the publisher:
Orchard Books, PO BOX 29, Douglas IM99 1BQ.
Credit card orders please telephone 01624 836000
or fax 01624 837033 or visit our website:
www.orchardbooks.co.uk
or e-mail: bookshop@enterprise.net for details.

To order please quote title, author and ISBN
and your full name and address.
Cheques and postal orders should be made
payable to 'Bookpost plc.'

Postage and packing is FREE within the UK
(overseas customers should add £2.00 per book).

Prices and availability are subject to change.